Wendell Phillips Garrison

Sonnets and Lyrics of the Ever-womanly

Wendell Phillips Garrison

Sonnets and Lyrics of the Ever-womanly

ISBN/EAN: 9783744770859

Printed in Europe, USA, Canada, Australia, Japan

Cover: Foto ©Andreas Hilbeck / pixelio.de

More available books at **www.hansebooks.com**

SONNETS
AND LYRICS OF THE
EVER–WOMANLY

Venne una Donna e disse : Io son Lucia.

Dante, Purg. ix.

PRIVATELY PRINTED
AT THE MARION PRESS, JAMAICA, NEW-YORK
FOR WENDELL PHILLIPS GARRISON
AND HIS FRIENDS
MDCCCXCVIII

TABLE.

SONNETS.

LYRICS.

PROTHALAMIUM.

How should we greet thee on thy bridal morn,
 This morn, that with extended hands cries "Take,
 Receive, accept!" ere it has cried "Awake!"?
Surely with gifts we greet thee: first, of corn,
For fruitfulness, along with Plenty's horn;
 And next, a Pan's-pipe from the reedy brake,
 For concord; lastly, for contentment's sake,
Of herbs a handful on a platter borne.
Thus dowered, and advancing with the day,
 Thy front all radiant and thy bosom free,
Oh look not back! nor think, "I must repay
 This bounty with my poor virginity."
Forward! nor heed the Voice that haunts the way:
 "This night thy soul shall be required of thee!"

Queste parole io riposi ne la mente con grande letizia, pensando di prenderle per mio cominciamento [finimento] : onde poi ritornato a la sopradetta cittade, e pensando alquanti di, cominciai una canzone con questo cominciamento [finimento].

        Dante, Vita Nuova, xix.

So young a thing to feel the tightening zone:
   And is her burden borne by wife or maid?
   What Faust, what casket, and what serenade
Of "Ring on Finger" of the Devil's own,
Have fruited thus? Or if in honor sown
   Her ripening increase beckons to the blade,
   Oh then might Juliet from her balustrade
Cast envious glances at her; from her throne,
The love-sick Dido; from her casement high,
   Hero, for her Leander blenched with doubt.—
Thus the poet muses as she passes by
   Heedless of him as of his prayer devout,
Nor marks the mood of pity in his eye:
   Who will be with her at her Crying-out?

Jam ut maxime jactes mihi virtutem bellicam, nemo vestrum, si semel esset expertus quid sit parere, non mallet decies in acie stare quam subire semel quod nobis toties est experiendum. In bello non semper venitur ad manus; . . . nobis cominus cum morte conflictandum est.

Erasmus, Colloquia: Puerpera.

When in thy glass thou studiest thy face,
  Not long, nor yet not seldom, half repelled
  And half attracted ; when thou hast beheld
Of Time's slow ravages the crumbling trace,
(Deciphered now with many an interspace
  The characters erewhile that Beauty spelled),
  And in thy throat a choking fear hath swelled
Of Love, grown cold, eluding thy embrace :
Could'st thou but read my gaze of tenderness —
  Affection fused with pity — precious tears
Would bring relief to thy unjust distress ;
  Thy visage, even as it to me appears,
Would seem to thee transfigured ; thou would'st bless
  Me, who am also, Dearest, scarred with years !

La mia donna fue immediata cagione di certe parole che nel sonetto sono, sì come appare a chi lo intende.

                                 Dante, Vita Nuova, vii.

Maria. — Fortassis alia tibi videbor ubi morbus aut ætas hanc formam immutarit.
Pampbilus. — Nec hoc corpus, o bona, semper erit æque succulentum. Sed ego non contemplor tantum istud undique florens et elegans domicilium ; hospitem magis adamo.

                         Erasmus, Colloquia : Proci et Puellæ.

Age can not wither her whom not gray hairs
    Nor furrowed cheeks have made the thrall of Time;
    For Spring lies.hidden under Winter's rime,
And violets know the victory is theirs.
Even so the corn of Egypt, unawares,
    Proud Nilus shelters with engulfing slime;
    So Etna's hardening crust a more sublime
Volley of pent-up fires at last prepares.
O face yet fair, if paler, and serene
    With sense of duty done without complaint!
O venerable crown!—a living green,
    Strength to the weak, and courage to the faint—
Thy bleaching locks, thy wrinkles, have but been
    Fresh beads upon the rosary of a saint!

A ministering angel thou.
        Scott, Marmion.

AT GREENWOOD CEMETERY.

Here was the ancient strand, the utmost reach,
  Of the great Northern ice-wave; hitherto
  With its last pulse it mounted, then withdrew,
Leaving its fringe of wreckage on the beach:
Boulder and pebble and sand-matrix — each
  From crag or valley ravished; scanty clue
  To its old site affording in its new,
Yet real, as the men of science teach.
Life hath not less its terminal moraine:
  Look how on that discharged from melting snows
Another rears itself, the spoil of plain
  And mountain also, marked by stones in rows,
With legend meet for such promiscuous pain:
  Here rests — Hier ruhet — or Ici repose.

Riposo alcun de le fatiche tante.
Petrarch, Son. cclxxix.

DENKMAL.

Memoriam quoque ipsam . . . "Memory too" . . .
   Cum voce . . . "with Expression" . . . (thus I read)
   Perdidissemus . . . "we had forfeited" . . .
Si tam in nostra potestate (rue
Is not more bitter than an if; yet who
   Begins must finish) *esset* (still a dread)
   Oblivisci quam tacere (O dear Head!   .
To think that I this knife-thrust must construe
In common English) . . . "if we could forget
   As easily as be silent."— Used was I
Indeed to silence; but when Age not yet
   Had blurred my mental tablets, tell me why
That firm memento of my grief I set
   Above the greensward where her ashes lie.

È ancor chi chiami, e non è chi responda.
            Petrarch, Son. cclxxvii.

THE ETHER MONUMENT.

Hotly they wrangle still, and still in vain
  Strive to adjudge the wreath, to carve the stone
  With one name only, his, however known,
Who taught an aching world to conquer Pain.
No Stoic I, to view them with disdain,
  And, callous to the universal moan
  Wrung from the agonies of flesh and bone,
To sigh for Roman fortitude again.
Yet the Soul's anguish craves a kindlier balm
  Than that death-aping drug, and otherwhere
I have found it and would fain bestow the palm:
  Yes, all that 's left of her who was so fair,
This image, moist with kissing—and this calm—
  I owe to thee, I owe to thee, Daguerre!

Morta è la donna tua, ch'era si bella.
       Dante, Vita Nuova, xxiii.

Dille : El basciar sie 'nvece di parole.
       Petrarch, Son. clxxiii.

REALITY.

Io non so s'egli è vero o s'e' mi pare . . .

Whether my fancy or the truth it be,
   I know not: in its frame her portrait turned
   Profile to full face on me, who had earned
This boon by deepest longing. You be free
To reject the miracle, and nothing see
   Save one poor brain that mused by fire that burned,
   And lids that feebly sleep's caresses spurned;
And write Illusion o'er my Verity.
I will not argue. Not more real I found
   Her condescension that she would be mine,
Those dear confiding arms which clasped me round,
   Or that immortal voice which, as with wine,
Quickened my pulse in words that still resound—
   "The kindliest eyes in all the world are thine!"

Ma la sua voce ancor quà giú rimbomba.
                 Petrarch, Son. lx.

ULTRA VIRES.

As in my sleep the niggard god of dreams
   Seldom thy phantom sends to me forlorn,
   Lost Fiordalisa! through his gate of horn,
(Pluto's half-brother, hardly less he seems
Implacable); so me from paltry themes
   The Muse diverts not, waking, nor with scorn
   Points from the sickly flames of marshes born
To that celestial Light which on me beams.
Wisely she hath refrained. Enough for me
   Humbly *the place, the time, the hour to bless*
That first my gaze was lifted unto thee,
   And for such honor to have thankfulness.
So far to follow Petrarch I am free;
   What after his could verse of mine express?

I' benedico il loco e 'l tempo e l'ora
Che sì alto miraron gli occhi mei,
E dico: "Anima, assai ringraziar dêi
Che fosti a tanto onor degnata allora."
                 Petrarch, Son. xii.

Je ne sçauroy, veu ma peine si forte,
Tant lamenter ne tant petrarchiser.
                 Ronsard.

27

MADONNA IN HEAVEN.

What day my Love passed on, around her pressed,
  With wonder filled and gentle sympathy,
  The elect of angels and the souls that be
The populace of heaven and therefore blest.
"What Light is this?" thus they themselves addressed,
  "And what new beauty? Form so gloriously
  Attired ne'er in this base century
Wandered from earth to this high place of rest."
But she, with her changed hostelry content,
  And peer of the most perfect, as it were
Expectant turns anon, with glances sent
  Backwards to see if I do follow her.
Hence all my thought and will on heaven is bent,
  Hearing her pray I be no loiterer.

      Li angeli eletti e l'anime beate
Cittadine del cielo, il primo giorno
Che Madonna passò, le fur intorno
Piene di meraviglia e di pietate.
      "Che luce è questa, e qual nova beltate?"
Dicean tra lor; "perch' abito sí adorno
Dal mondo errante a quest' alto soggiorno
Non sali mai in tutta questa etate."
      Ella, contenta aver cangiato albergo,
Si paragona pur coi piú perfetti;
E, parte, ad or ad or si volge a tergo,
      Mirando s'io la seguo, e par ch'aspetti:
Ond'io voglie e pensier tutti al ciel ergo,
Perch'i' l'odo pregar pur ch'i' m'affretti.

Petrarch, Son. ccc.

VALCHIUSA REVISITED.

I feel my old-time breeze; before me loom
  The endearèd hills native to that fair Light
  Which kept mine eyes, Heaven willing, eager-bright,
Now only keeps them filled with tears and gloom.
Oh foolish thoughts! oh hopes consigned to doom!
  Tinged are the streams, and on the grass a blight,
  And cold and empty the nest whence she took flight,
Wherein I live, and would have had my tomb,
  Hoping her beauteous eyes (that did my breast
  Consume) and delicate footprints might afford
At last from so great weariness some rest.
  Served have I a cruel and a stingy lord;
For I was racked while I my flame possessed—
  Now is my grief o'er scattered embers poured.

    Sento l'aura mia antica, e i dolci colli
Veggio apparire onde 'l bel lume nacque
Che tenne gli occhi mei, mentr' al ciel piacque,
Bramosi e lieti, or li tên tristi e molli.
    Oh caduche speranze! oh penser folli!
Vedove l'erbe e torbide son l'acque,
E vôto e freddo il nido in ch' ella giacque,
Nel qual io vivo, e morto giacer volli,
    Sperando alfin da le soavi piante
E da' belli occhi suoi, che 'l cor m' hann' arso,
Riposo alcun de le fatiche tante.
    Ho servito a signor crudele e scarso;
Ch' arsi quanto 'l mio foco ebbi davante;
Or vo piangendo il suo cenere sparso.

Petrarch, *Son.* cclxxix.

SUPPLICATION.

I go lamenting that in vanished days
  I chose to love a perishable thing,
  Nor soared aloft, though having strength of wing
Haply to no mean levels me to raise.
Thou who my unmerited lot and grievous ways
  Seest, unseen and deathless Heavenly King!
  Succor a frail soul in its wandering,
And of Thy grace replenish its decays.
That so, if I have lived in storm and stress,
  I die in port and peace; and, vain my stay,
That I at least depart with comeliness.
  For my small remnant of life vouchsafe, I pray,
Thy hand be near, and when I die not less:
  Of hope in others Thou knowest I have no ray.

I' vo piangendo i miei passati tempi,
I quai pósi in amar cosa mortale,
Senza levarmi a volo, abbiend' io l'ale
Per dar forse di me non bassi esempi.
  Tu, che vedi i miei mali indegni ed empi,
Re del cielo, invisible, immortale,
Soccorri a l'alma disviata e frale,
E 'l suo defetto di tua grazia adempi:
  Sì che, s'io vissi in guerra ed in tempesta,
Mora in pace ed in porto; e, se la stanza
Fu vana, almen sia la partita onesta.
  A quel poco di viver che m'avanza
Ed al morir degni esser tua man presta:
Tu sai ben che 'n altrui non ho speranza.

Petrarch, Son. cccxvii.

LYRICS.

Fuor' i biondi capelli allor velati.

MONOCHROME.

Her let me not despise who doth admire
   The sun's hue, and the cowslip's, and the bee's,
Amber, and brass, the oriole's attire,
   And China's ensign in the Yellow Seas!

Haply the odious vesture of her race
   Of old from out her mirror flung a sheen
Of glory o'er some swart Rebekah's face,—
   And broad the Ghetto grew that close had been;

Or poor Selvaggia something less profound
   Felt in her soul the deeps of her despair,
Though for a fleeting instant, as she wound
   The shameful riband in her raven hair.

. . . The badge which was least in honor in the Middle Ages.
Yellow was the badge to which the Jew was condemned. It was a
yellow cap that marked out the son of the Ghetto for the scorn of
the street urchin. Yellow was the color of shame and of shameless
womanhood. . . . "Saffron is the badge of all our tribe."

I. Zangwill.

MORITURA.

Constant I, but thou art changed :
   Time and Death, for our undoing,
Old affection have estranged,
   Put an end to lovers' wooing.

I am constant : though thy tongue,
   Unsheathed sword, doth pierce me thorough,
Thought of what thou wast when young
   Turns to joy my present sorrow.

Thou art changed : so advertise
   Halting pulse and nerves aquiver,
Want of lustre in thine eyes,
   Life returning to its Giver.

Di memoria e di speme il cor pascendo.
             Petrarch, Canz. xxvi.

PHAROS.

Aloof I dote on thy sunshiny locks,
  Lady ! for in thy unimpassioned eye
I read too well the coast-light's paradox:
  A friend — but come not nigh !

                      Certe extrema linea
         Amare haud nil est.
                        Terence, Eunuchus.

INDEX TO FIRST LINES.